MY FAMILY, YOUR FAMILY, OUR FAMILIES

By EMMA CARLSON BERNE
Illustrations by JOANIE STONE
Music by MARK OBLINGER

CANTATA LEARNING

WWW.CANTATALEARNING.COM

CANTATA
LEARNING

Published by Cantata Learning
1710 Roe Crest Drive
North Mankato, MN 56003
www.cantatalearning.com

Library of Congress Cataloging-in-Publication Data
Names: Berne, Emma Carlson, author. | Stone, Joanie, illustrator. | Oblinger, Mark, composer.
Title: My family, your family, our families / by Emma Carlson Berne ; illustrations by Joanie Stone ; music by Mark Oblinger.
Description: North Mankato, MN : Cantata Learning, 2019. | Series: How are we alike and different? | Audience: K to Grade 3.
Identifiers: LCCN 2017056295 (print) | LCCN 2018002224 (ebook) | ISBN 9781684102631 (eBook) | ISBN 9781684102372 (hardcover) | ISBN 9781684102891 (paperback)
Subjects: LCSH: Families--Cross-cultural studies.
Classification: LCC HQ744 (ebook) | LCC HQ744 .B46 2018 (print) | DDC 306.85--dc23
LC record available at https://lccn.loc.gov/2017056295

Book design and art direction, Tim Palin Creative
Editorial direction, Kellie M. Hultgren
Music direction, Elizabeth Draper
Music arranged and produced by Mark Oblinger

ACCESS THE MUSIC!
SCAN CODE WITH MOBILE APP
CANTATALEARNING.COM

Printed in the United States 6208

TIPS TO SUPPORT LITERACY AT HOME

WHY READING AND SINGING WITH YOUR CHILD IS SO IMPORTANT

Daily reading with your child leads to increased academic achievement. Music and songs, specifically rhyming songs, are a fun and easy way to build early literacy and language development. Music skills correlate significantly with both phonological awareness and reading development. Singing helps build vocabulary and speech development. And reading and appreciating music together is a wonderful way to strengthen your relationship.

READ AND SING EVERY DAY!

TIPS FOR USING CANTATA LEARNING BOOKS AND SONGS DURING YOUR DAILY STORY TIME

1. As you sing and read, point out the different words on the page that rhyme. Suggest other words that rhyme.
2. Memorize simple rhymes such as Itsy Bitsy Spider and sing them together. This encourages comprehension skills and early literacy skills.
3. Use the questions in the back of each book to guide your singing and storytelling.
4. Read the included sheet music with your child while you listen to the song. How do the music notes correlate to the words of the song?
5. Sing along on the go and at home. Access music by scanning the QR code on each Cantata book. You can also stream or download the music for free to your computer, smartphone, or mobile device.

Devoting time to daily reading shows that you are available for your child. Together, you are building language, literacy, and listening skills.

Have fun reading and singing!

Just like there are **different** kinds of people all over the world, there are also different kinds of families. A family might be a mother and father and two or three children. A family might be grandparents, parents, aunts, uncles, and cousins all living in one house. A family might be two moms or two dads, or just one parent and one child! Families are full of love and **caring**, no matter how different they are from each other. Let's sing together about families!

This is my mother. This is my father.
We live together in one place.

I have a brother. Here is my sister.
All as one, we share this space.

S
P

Families are made up of special people.
Some have many. Some have few.

They share a home,
and they help each other.
Families care for me and you.

My house is home to a lot of people:
Mom and Dad and Nana, too.

My grandpa lives here. So does my auntie.
And my **cousins**? I have a few.

Families are made up of special people.
Some have many. Some have few.

They share a home, and they help each other.
Families care for me and you.

My family has just three people in it:
me and Grandma and Granddad.

My friend, he lives with his foster mother.
She gives him hugs when he is sad.

Families are made up of special people.
Some have many. Some have few.

They share a home, and they help each other.
Families care for me and you.

My mom lives with me. My dad lives **elsewhere**. We have two homes where we belong.

Sometimes it's hard, but we love each other and we keep our family strong.

2038

Families are made up of special people.
Some have many. Some have few.

They share a home, and they help each other.
Families care for me and you.

They share a home, and they help each other.
Families care for me and you.
Families care for me and you.

SONG LYRICS

My Family, Your Family, Our Families

This is my mother. This is my father.
We live together in one place.
I have a brother. Here is my sister.
All as one, we share this space.

Families are made up of special people.
Some have many. Some have few.
They share a home, and they help each other.
Families care for me and you.

My house is home to a lot of people:
Mom and Dad and Nana, too.
My grandpa lives here. So does my auntie.
And my cousins? I have a few.

Families are made up of special people.
Some have many. Some have few.
They share a home, and they help each other.
Families care for me and you.

My family has just three people in it:
me and Grandma and Granddad.
My friend, he lives with his foster mother.
She gives him hugs when he is sad.

Families are made up of special people.
Some have many. Some have few.
They share a home, and they help each other.
Families care for me and you.

My mom lives with me. My dad lives elsewhere.
We have two homes where we belong.
Sometimes it's hard, but we love each other
and we keep our family strong.

Families are made up of special people.
Some have many. Some have few.
They share a home, and they help each other.
Families care for me and you.

They share a home and help each other.
Families care for me and you.
Families care for me and you.

My Family, Your Family, Our Families

World
Mark Oblinger

Verse 2
My house is home to a lot of people:
Mom and Dad and Nana, too.
My grandpa lives here. So does my auntie.
And my cousins? I have a few.

Chorus

Verse 3
My family has just three people in it:
me and Grandma and Granddad.
My friend, he lives with his foster mother.
She gives him hugs when he is sad.

Chorus

Verse 4
My mom lives with me. My dad lives elsewhere.
We have two homes where we belong.
Sometimes it's hard, but we love each other
and we keep our family strong.

Chorus

GLOSSARY

caring—helping and loving others

cousins—the children of an aunt or uncle

different—not the same

elsewhere—in some other place, not here

CRITICAL THINKING QUESTIONS

1. This song talks about different kinds of families. Draw a picture of your own family. Who lives with you?
2. Do you know someone who lives in a different sort of family than yours? What is that person's family like?
3. Can you think of a type of family that is not described in this song? Describe this type of family in your own way.

TO LEARN MORE

Harris, Robie H. *Who's in My Family? All About Our Families*. Somerville, MA: Candlewick Press, 2012.

Parr, Todd. *The Family Book*. New York: Little, Brown, 2010.

Ruurs, Margriet. *Families Around the World*. Toronto, ON: Kids Can Press, 2017.